Wherever You Go

by Pat Zietlow Miller

illustrated by Eliza Wheeler

LITTLE, BROWN AND COMPANY

New York   Boston

When it's time for a journey, to learn and to grow,
roads guide your footsteps wherever you go.
Roads give you chances to seek and explore.
Want an adventure?

Just open your door.

*R*oads...go.
Over a hill,
under a bridge,
deep in a valley,
high on a ridge.

If you yearn for the ocean or wish for a stream,
roads bring you closer to reaching your dream.

Roads...zoom.
Beneath city buildings
that tower on high,
twinkling like stars
in the dark velvet sky.

Racing past signs.
Reflecting their light.
Zigging and zagging.
Turn left. Then turn right.

Roads...bend.
Detours head where
you wouldn't expect,
showing you various ways to connect.

Bringing you closer,
then curving away.
You always have choices.
To go?
Or to stay?

*R*oads...reach.
Across flowing rivers,
past harbors and bays,
with breathtaking bridges
designed to amaze.

Attaching two places that once were apart.
Choose to cross over.
Follow your heart.

*R*oads...*merge.*
*S*mall, distant roads sometimes travel alone,
marking the miles out there on their own.

Then a new road wants to join in the fun,
heads the same way, and the two become one.

Roads...grow.
Well-traveled roads sometimes need extra space
to guide life's adventurers to a new place.

Which path should you choose?
That's easy to see.
The one that will take you
where you wish to be.

Roads...wait.
For click-clacking trains
and boats with tall *sails.*
Slow-going hay wagons carrying bales.

Stoplights and crosswalks,
a deer with a friend.
Roads sometimes pause,
or just come to an end.

Roads...climb.
Steep mountain peaks dusted lightly with snow,
rising above the deep canyon below.

Clinging to cliffs.
Chasing a cloud.
Reaching the top,
tired but proud.

Roads...remember.
Every life landmark, the big and the small.
The moments you tripped,
the times you stood tall.

Where you are going, and where you began.
What you expected. What you didn't plan.

Roads...return.

During your journey, you'll ramble and roam.

But sooner or later, you'll think of your home.

After you've seen all you needed to see,

a road takes you back where you're longing to be.

Back to that hill,
under that bridge,
deep in your valley,
high on your ridge.

Roads take you all over the planet, but then...

you always can follow them home once again.

To Gwen: May the roads you choose in life
lead you exactly where you wish to be.

–PZM

A book for Audrey.

–EW

About This Book

The illustrations for this book were done with dip pens and India ink and colored with watercolors and gouache on Arches watercolor paper. The text was set in Nicolas Cochin, and the display type was hand-lettered by Sasha Prood.

This book was edited by Connie Hsu and Leslie Shumate and designed by Patti Ann Harris. The production was supervised by Erika Schwartz, and the production editor was Christine Ma.

• Little, Brown and Company • Hachette Book Group • 1290 Avenue of the Americas, New York, NY 10104 • Visit our website at lb-kids.com • Little, Brown and Company is a division of Hachette Book Group, Inc. • The Little, Brown name and logo are trademarks of Hachette Book Group, Inc. • The publisher is not responsible for websites (or their content) that are not owned by the publisher. • First Edition: May 2015 • Library of Congress Cataloging-in-Publication Data • Miller, Pat Zietlow. • Wherever you go / by Pat Zietlow Miller ; illustrated by Eliza Wheeler.—First edition. • pages cm • Summary: Illustrations and rhyming text follow a young rabbit as he leaves home on a journey, discovering the joys of different kinds of roads and what they may bring—including a way back home. • ISBN 978-0-316-40002-2 (hardcover) • [1. Stories in rhyme. 2. Roads—Fiction. 3. Voyages and travels—Fiction. 4. Rabbits—Fiction.] I. Wheeler, Eliza, illustrator. II. Title. • PZ8.3.M6183Whe 2015 • [E]—dc23 • 2013039354 • 10 9 8 7 6 5 • APS • Printed in China